VIZ PREMIERE COMICS

Crying freeman

Story by
KAZUO KOIKE
Art by
RYOICHI IKEGAMI

Story by Kazuo Koike
Art by Ryoichi Ikegami

◉

Original Japanese Version
Editor-in-chief/Yonosuke Konishi (Shogakukan, Inc.)
Executive Editor/Katsuya Shirai (Shogakukan, Inc.)

◉

English Version
Translation/Gerard Jones, Will Jacobs, & Satoru Fujii
Touch Up Art & Lettering/Wayne Truman
Cover Design/Viz Graphics
Editors/Jerry A. Novick & John Togashi
Executive Editor/Seiji Horibuchi
Publisher/Masahiro Oga

◉

◉

Published by Viz Comics
P.O. Box 77010, San Francisco, CA 94107

CHAPTER 1
MR. YO PART 16

CHK

SSSS

SKCH

Oh!

TUP

PAH

KCH

TELL ME WHO KILLED THEM.

A--A-- M-MAFIA GANG.

GOOD. NOW CALL THE POLICE.

Y-YES, SIR.

REMEMBER... YOU AND I ARE THE ONLY WITNESSES.

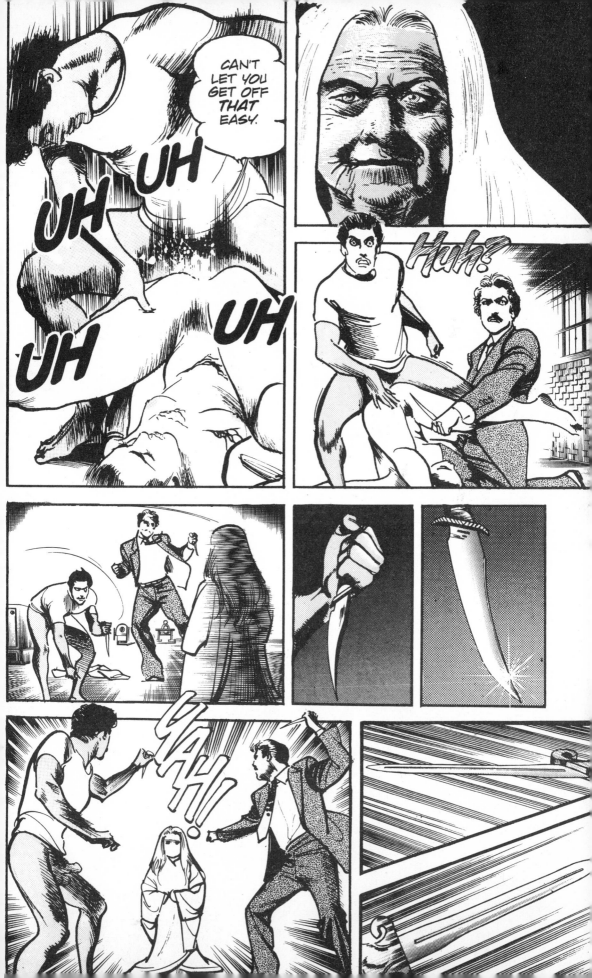

MY FIRST TARGET HAS PERISHED INSTANTLY.

MY SECOND HAS, I BELIEVE, SOME TWO HOURS LEFT TO LIVE.

FOLLOW HIM, FREEMAN. WHEN A MAN IS OVERWHELMED BY THE FEAR OF DEATH, HE RUNS TO SOMEONE WHO WILL HELP HIM. THAT SOMEONE WILL BELONG TO **CAMORA.**

IF YOU STRIKE THAT SOMEONE SO THAT **HE** WILL LIVE FOR TWO HOURS MORE... THEN HE WILL LEAD YOU TO THE NEXT MAN.

THUS YOU CAN FOLLOW A TRAIL OF BLOOD UNTIL IT FINALLY ENDS... AT THE LOCAL **BOSS** OF **CAMORA.**

DESTROY **THAT** MAN... AND CAMORA'S ORGANIZATION IN HONG KONG COMES TO ITS END.

NOW GO, FREEMAN. **GO.**

END CAMORA'S ORGANIZATION-- BY YOURSELF.

Hah

17

WELL DONE, SHI ENJU. YOU NETTED THOSE AGENTS OF CAMORA QUITE IMPRESSIVELY.

I FORGIVE YOU YOUR TRANSGRESSION.

DO NOT DIE, SHI ENJU... UNTIL FREEMAN RETURNS.

I SHALL ALLOW YOU TO COMPLETE FREEMAN'S TATTOOS WITH YOUR OWN HAND... AND MARK THEM WITH YOUR SIGN.

I... I AM GLAD...

HELP ME...
I'VE...
I'VE BEEN
ATTACKED...
I'M... I'M...

EEK

VSSHH

CHAPTER 1
MR. YO PART 15

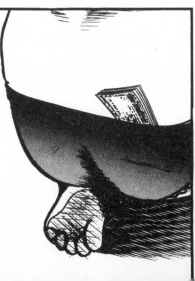

WHA--?

CHUK

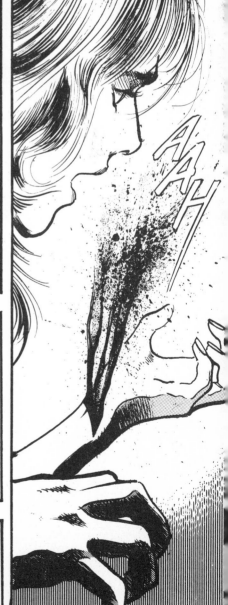

AAH

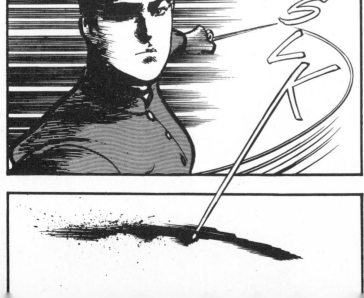

SSK

WHAT
IS
IT?

YOU DIDN'T SEE THIS. UNDER-STAND?

I... I...

AND YOU'LL FORGET MY FACE.

Y-YES...

YOU'RE VERY BEAUTIFUL. WITH A LITTLE PRU-DENCE...YOU'LL REMAIN SO.

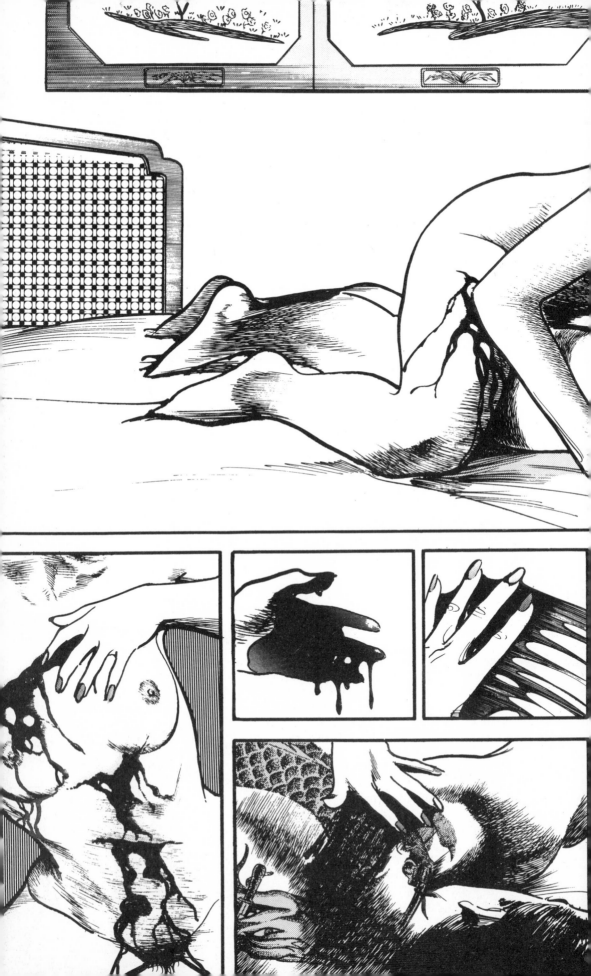

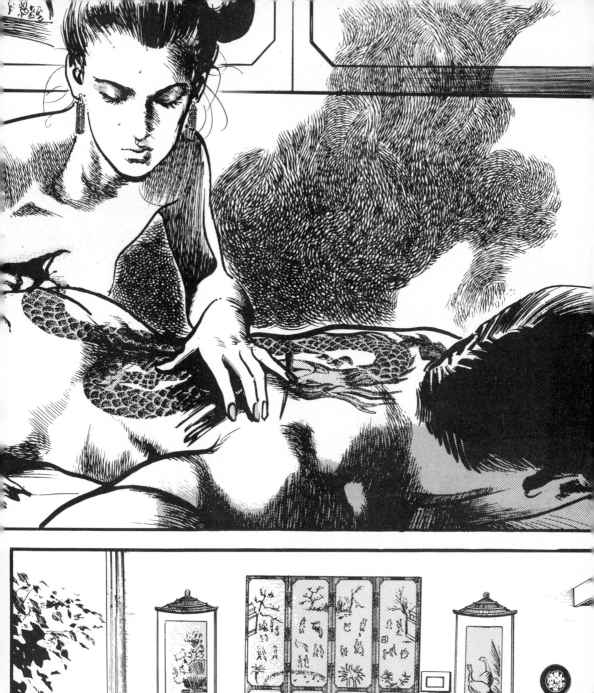

IF YOU BECOME AN ASSASSIN WHO CAN MAKE ALLIES OF ALL WOMEN... THEN YOU SHALL LIVE FOREVER.

NOW, RETURN TO JAPAN. AS YO HINOMURA.

CHAPTER 1
MR. YO PART 14

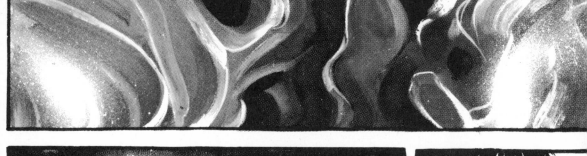

WHY DO I CRY ? I DON'T KNOW.

PERHAPS IT'S ONLY FROM RELIEF... THAT THE KILLING IS DONE... THAT I'M FREE FROM THE KEYWORDS... THAT FREEMAN CAN BECOME YO HINOMURA ONCE AGAIN.

WHATEVER THE REASON, MY TEARS HAVE EARNED ME THIS... *IRONIC* NAME. "CRYING FREEMAN."

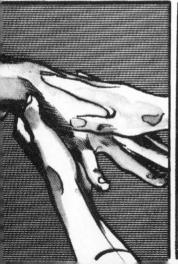

新聞定価1ヵ月2,800円・1部売り(朝刊)80円(夕刊)40円

白真会会長を殺した
殺し屋をはっきり目撃した
カミソリ竜二こと
花山竜二氏が激白‼

CONFESSIONS OF
RYUJI "THE BLADE"
HANAYAMA

"I SAW THE
HAKUSHIN
KILLER!"

週刊ポスト 250円

AND
HERE'S
ANOTHER
LITTLE
TIDBIT.

おれは地獄の、底まであの野郎を追いかけてぶっ殺してやる

会長の仇は必ず討つと誓う

カミソリ竜二!!

"BLADE" SWEARS VENGEANCE ON ASSASSIN

"I'LL HUNT HIM TO THE PITS OF HELL!"

HE'S BAITING THE TRAP.

SETTING YOU UP.

BUT HE *IS* THE WITNESS. I HAVE NO CHOICE.

THEN I'LL GET READY.

EMU...WHY DON'T YOU STAY HERE? NONE OF THE LOCAL PEOPLE WILL SEE ANYTHING STRANGE IN THAT.

A MAN NAMED MURATA IS COMING FROM TOKYO TO BUY SOME OF MY WORK. HE KNOWS NOTHING OF FREEMAN...AND THINKS OF YO HINOMURA AS HIS BEST FRIEND.

I'LL CALL HIM, TELL HIM YOU'LL BE SELLING MY PIECES, ONE BY ONE. YOU CAN MAKE A LIVING THAT WAY.

BUT YOU MUST *NOT* LEAVE WEST IZU.

YOU'LL BE SAFE... AS LONG AS YOU ARE HERE.

BUT... WHAT IF YOU DON'T COME BACK?

LIVE YOUR OWN LIFE.

YOU WON'T NEED ME. YOU CAN USE THIS KILN TO MAKE POTTERY OF YOUR OWN.

YOU HAVE AN ENORMOUS TALENT, EMU. I CAN SEE IT IN YOU.

YOU'RE LEAVING ME, AREN'T YOU?

YOU NEVER EXPECT TO COME BACK-- DO YOU?

WHY DO YOU THINK I CONFESSED MY PAST TO YOU? YOU HAVE TO UNDER- STAND...

I AM *CRYING FREEMAN*!

COME BACK TO ME... PLEASE. IF YOU DON'T RETURN IN TEN DAYS, I...

I'LL GO TO TOKYO! TO HONG KONG! I'LL FIND YOU!

BRRRM...

WHEN THIS IS DONE, YOU OUGHT'TA GO BACK. I THINK SHE'S ALL RIGHT.

YOU COULD TATTOO TIGERS ON HER. YOU KNOW? SHE'S THE KIND OF WOMAN A DRAGON NEEDS.

YEAH. SHE'S THE REAL STUFF.

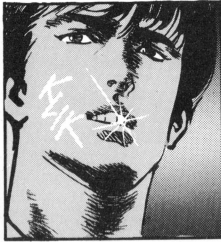

tink

WE'RE WITH THE 108 DRAGONS.

MR. DOGAKI, IF RYUJI HANAYAMA DIES, YOU TAKE OVER THE HAKUSHIN. RIGHT?

SO WHAT DO YOU DO? PLAY BALL? OR LEAVE YOUR GIRLFRIEND SCREWING A CORPSE?

FFK

MY FRIEND HERE KILLED SHUDO SHIMAZAKI.

T-TELL ME WHAT TO DO.

OFFICE OF THE HANADA FAMILY

RRRNG

BOSS? IT'S MR. DOGAKI.

IT'S ME.

YOU'LL *WHAT*?

I'LL SEND YOU FIVE MILLION YEN... AND TWO OF MY BOYS. USE THEM AS YOU WANT.

THEY'RE BOTH PRETTY TOUGH.

YOU'LL KNOW ONE BY HIS GOLD TOOTH AND HIS DARK GLASSES-- THAT'S *NOMURA*.

THANKS FOR THE OFFER. BUT NO THANKS.

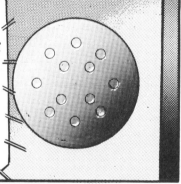

IF YOU REFUSE MY GIFT, IT WOULD MAKE ME APPEAR DISLOYAL... YOU ARE, AFTER ALL, THE HAKUSHIN'S NEW CHAIRMAN.

heh

OKAY. SEND THEM.

58

TO BE CONTINUED

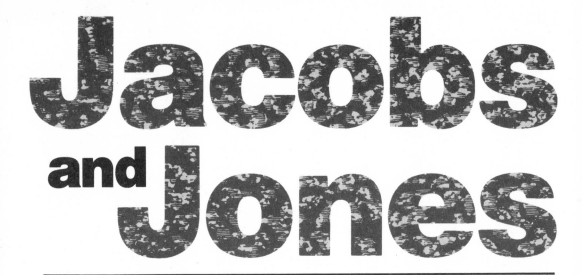

Jacobs and Jones

The Collaboration Continues

Two young novelists meet while working at a used bookstore. Their early acquaintanceship is, naturally, marked by much intellectual strutting and jousting. One champions the mimetic fictionalization of personal experience. The other propounds semiotic explorations through the reinvention of ancient myths. They butt heads a bit, they drink a bit, they never quite break the ice.

Come summer, there is a comic book convention in San Francisco. One of our young novelists, secure in the belief that no one he knows will ever see him there, seizes the opportunity to add to his secret cache of old *Green Lantern* and *Hawkman* comics. He has just gleefully purchased a copy of "Menace of the Dragonfly Raiders" when he turns a corner and

. . .what does he see?

Only his fellow young hyperliterate strolling toward him with a huge stack of *Iron Man* under his arm.

Will Jacobs and Gerard Jones were faced with a choice in that moment: one of them could kill the other. . .or they could become partners. Having learned from the example of the super heroes whom they idolized, they inevitably chose the latter course.

Since 1978, these two have tried to walk a fine line between Art and Junk, between seriously-intended comments on the world and raucous pop culture. Over and over again, they've had to cling to each other for balance. In 1983 their shared schizophrenia exploded into humor, in the form of a book called *The Beaver Papers;* it sold well, garnered a great deal of media attention, and convinced the erstwhile literary wannabees that they should probably be writing together.

A stint on *The National Lampoon* followed, and then the creation of their favorite work: *The Trouble with Girls,* a comic book filled with bizarre characters and inverted cliches and assorted satires (now being developed as a movie by 20th Century Fox, with a screenplay by the creators). In early 1989, however, in the midst of taking *Girls* from one publisher to another, they found themselves trapped in a brief hiatus. They cast about for some way to fill the time while continuing to work together; and *Crying Freeman* appeared.

This was a welcome chance to collaborate on something other than humor. Jacobs and Jones had written a couple of mystery novels, but neither had seen print. Gerard had already lined up quite a bit of serious comic book work *(The Shadow Strikes, Green Lantern,* and *El Diablo,* all from DC). And Will was hard at work on a novel of his own. But *Freeman* has enabled them to combine their abilities in rewriting some intense, and not very humorous, material.